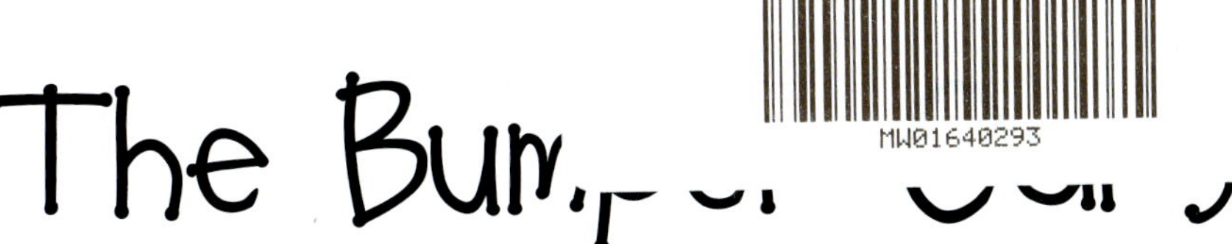

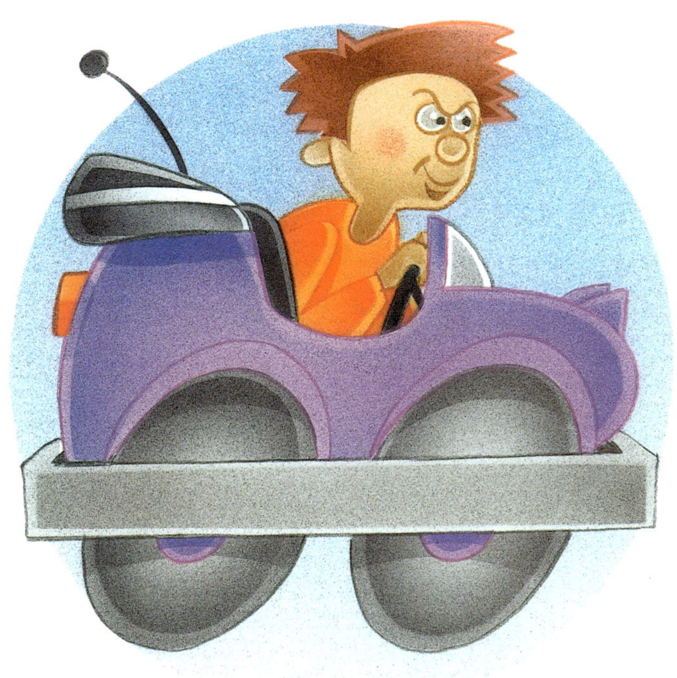

Illustrated by Martin Bailey

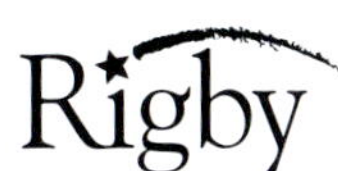

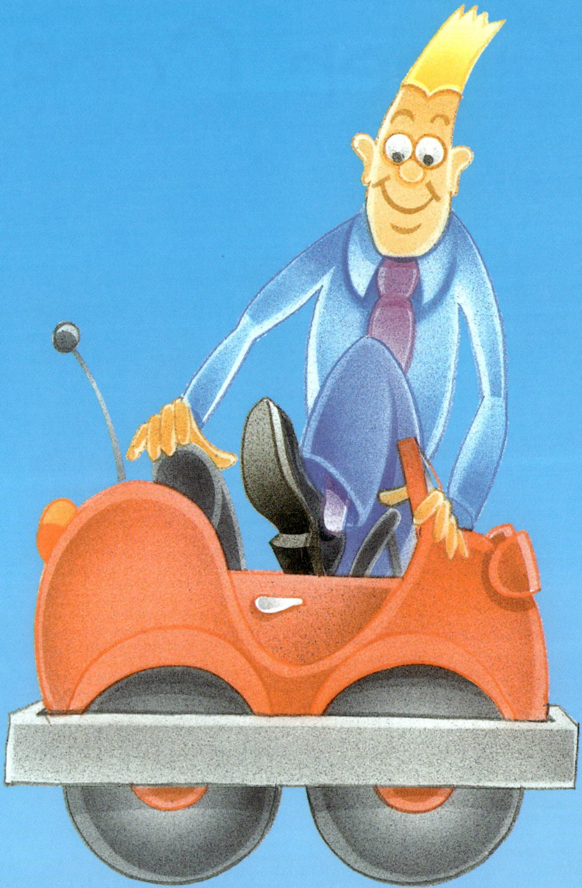

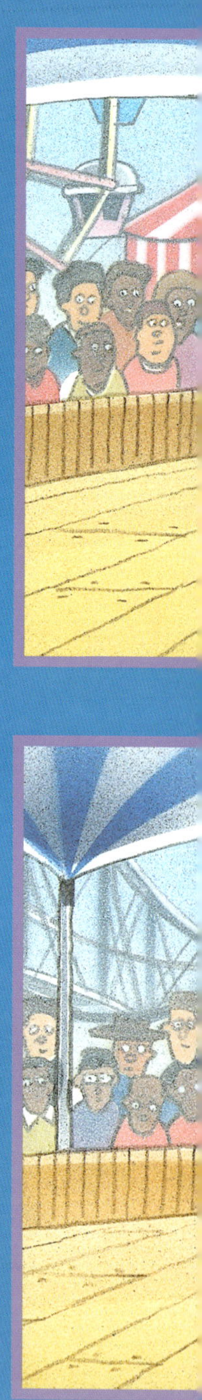

The red car
is for me.

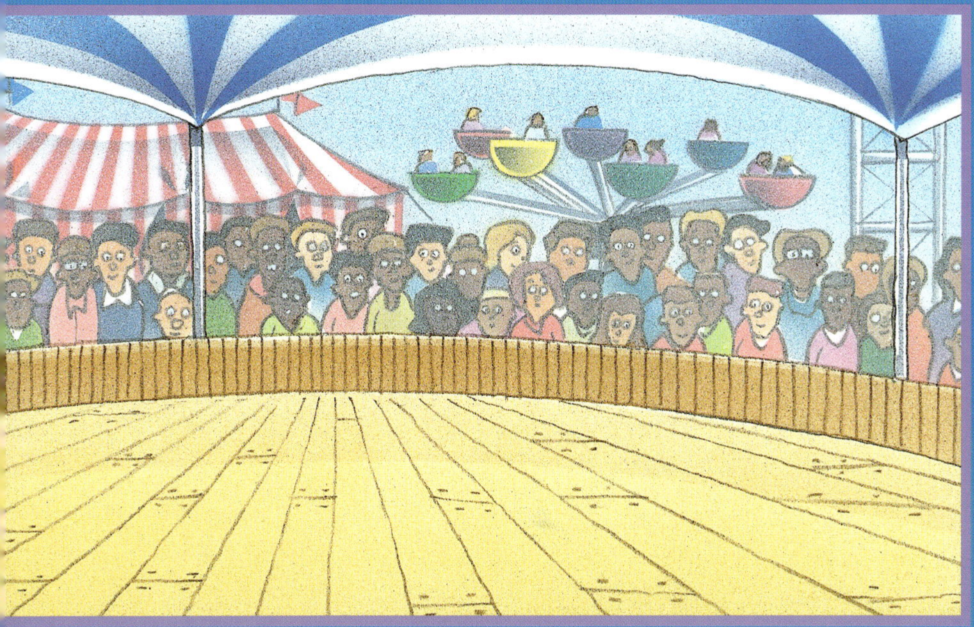

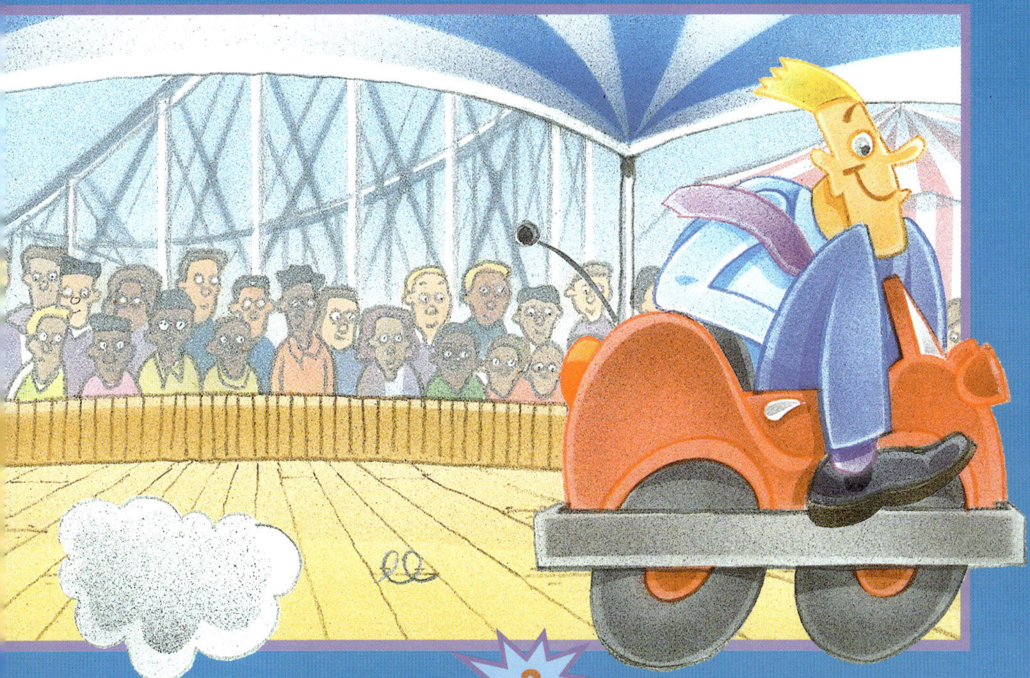

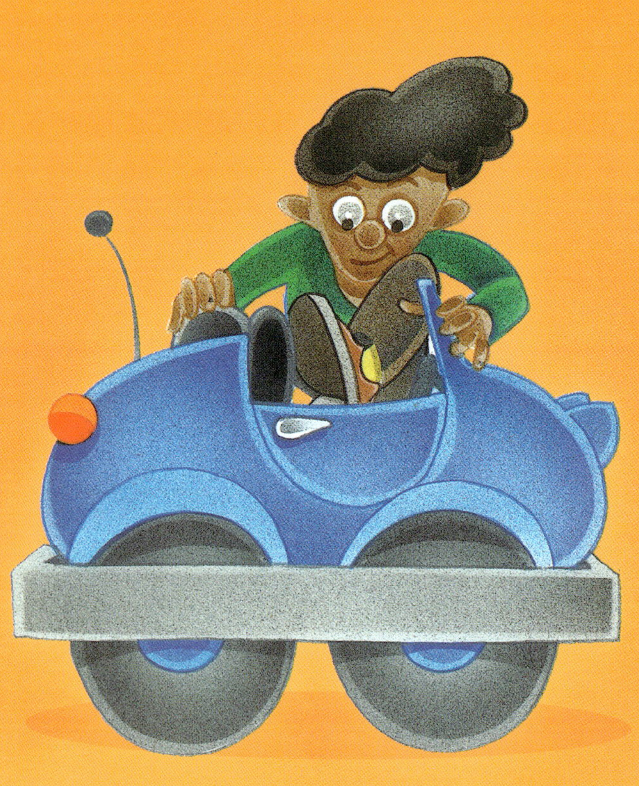

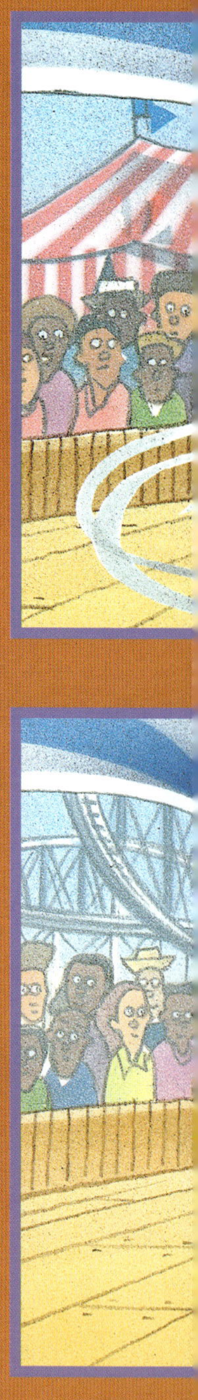

The blue car
is for me.

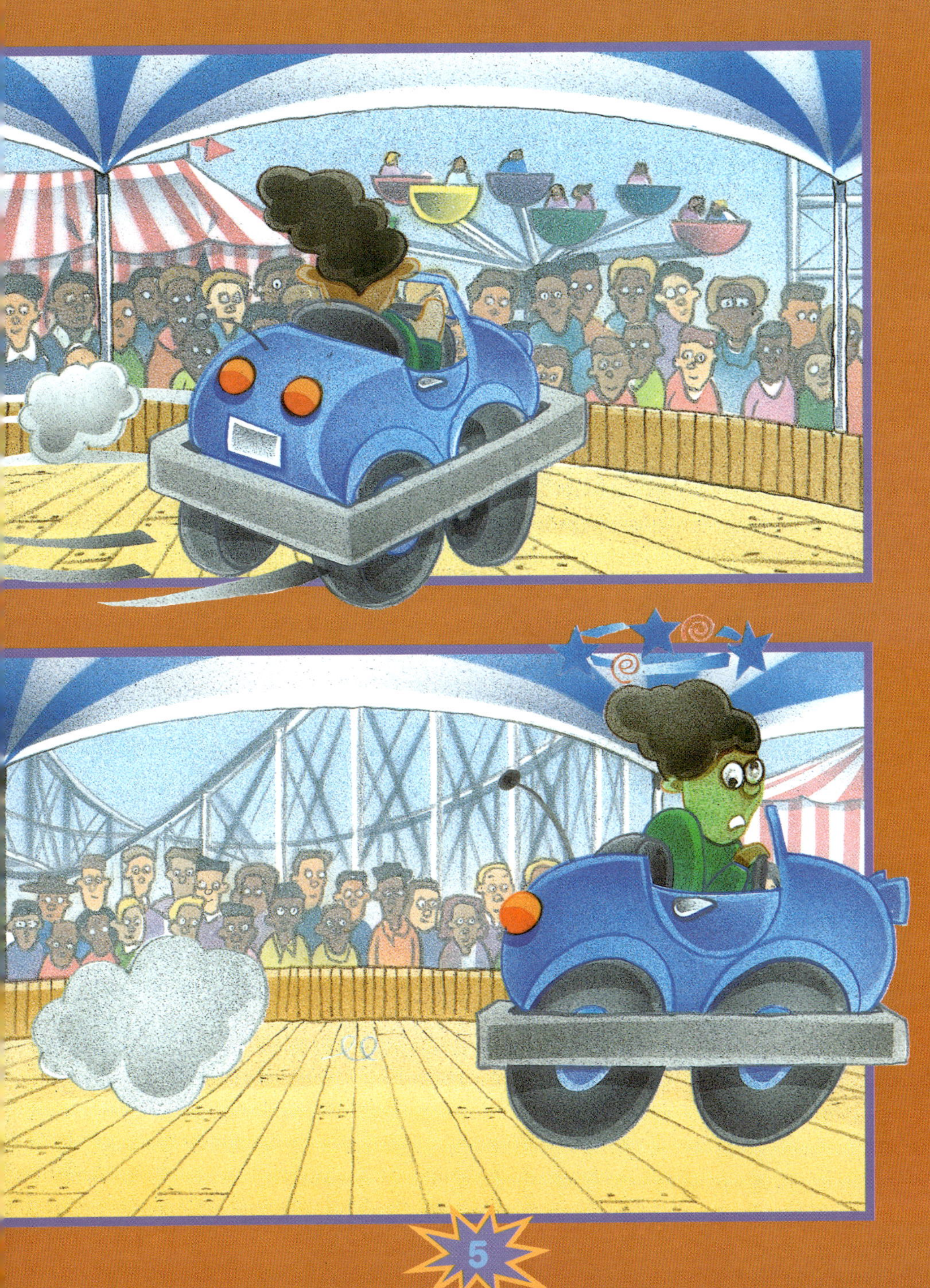

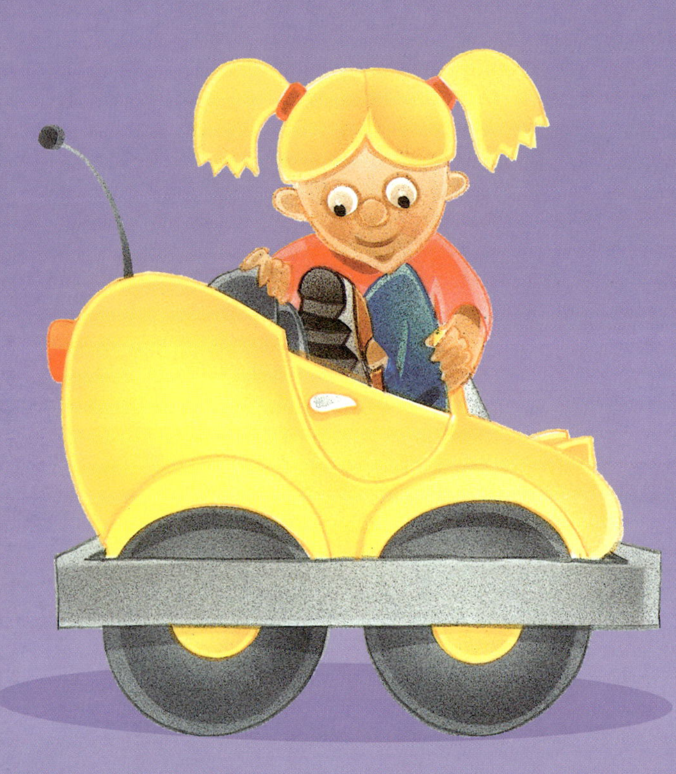

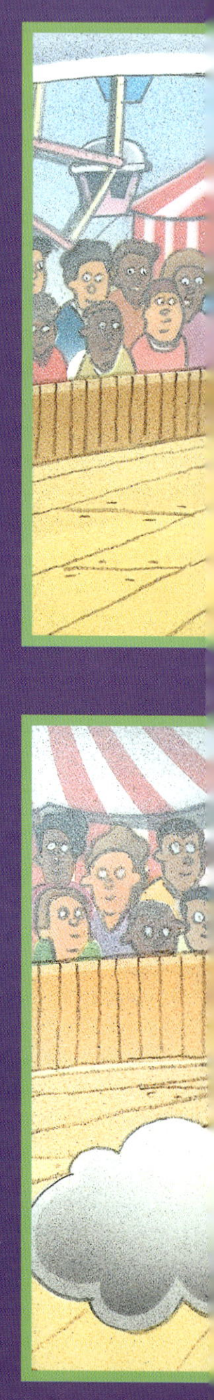

The yellow car
is for me.

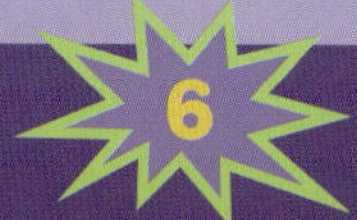

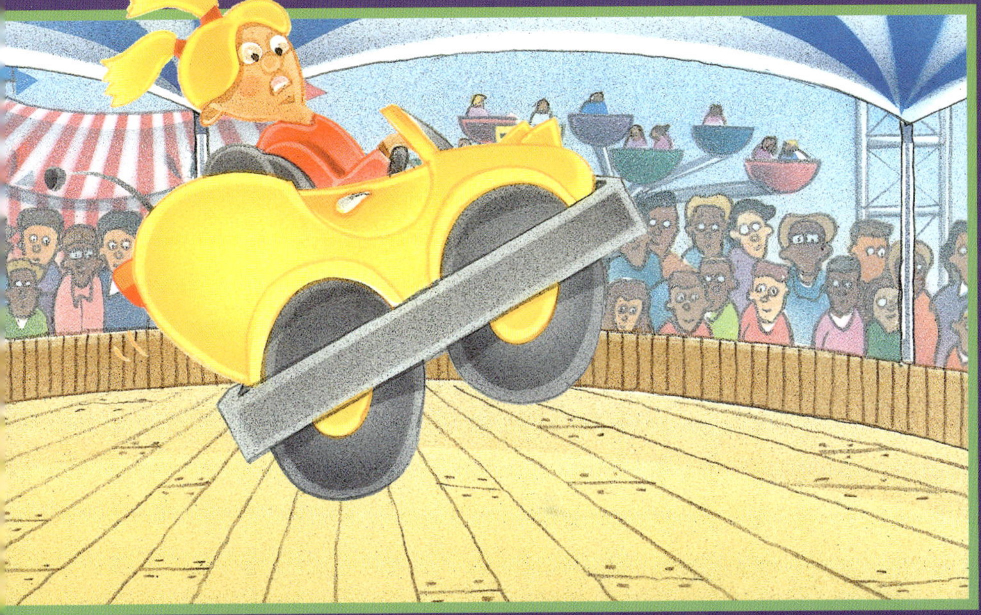

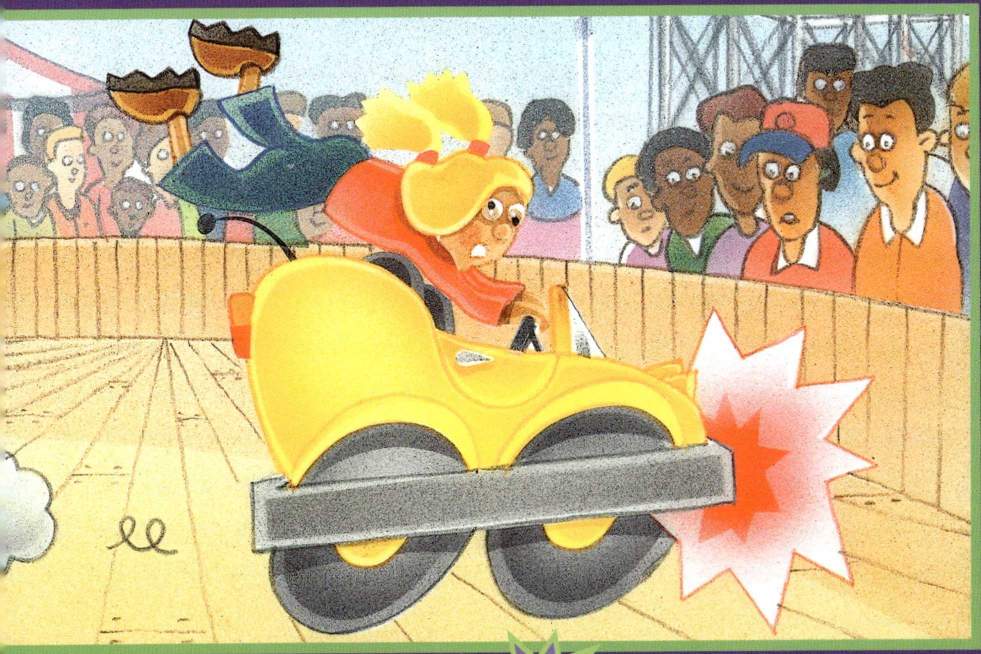

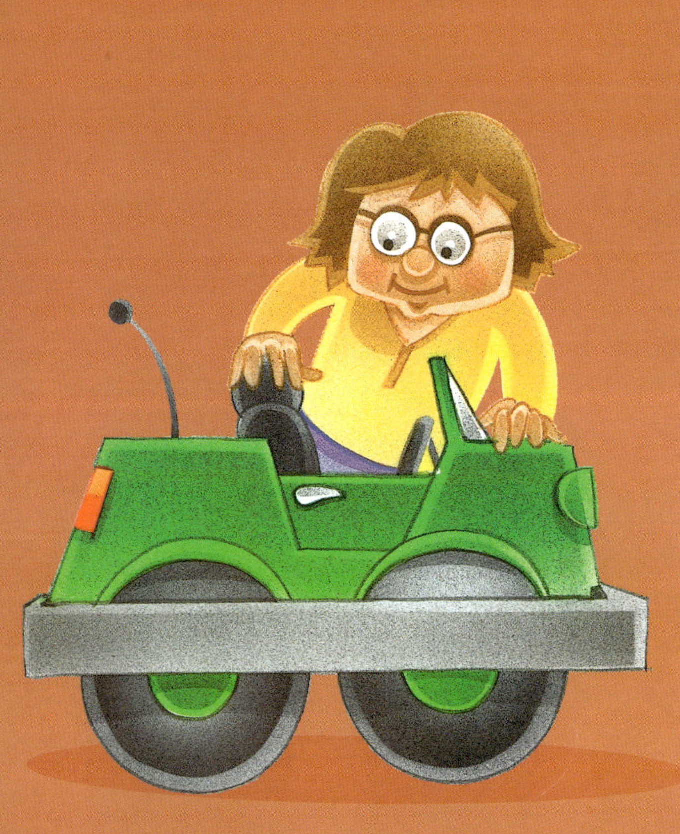

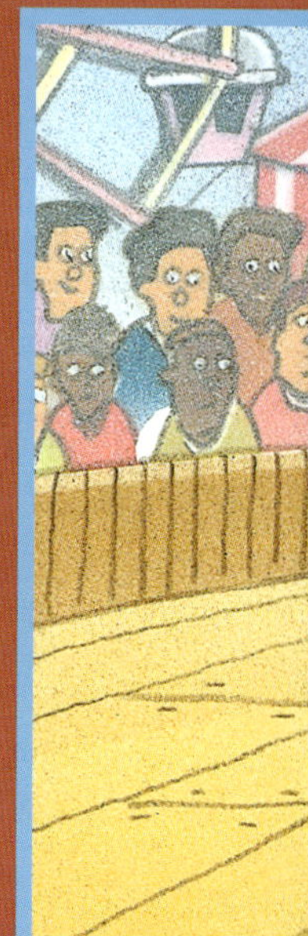

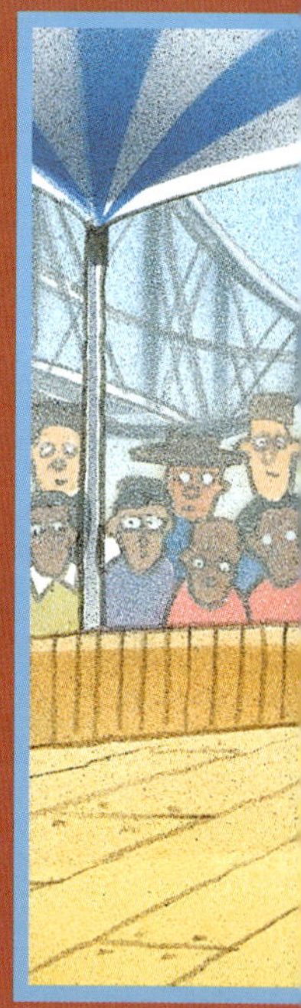

The green car
is for me.

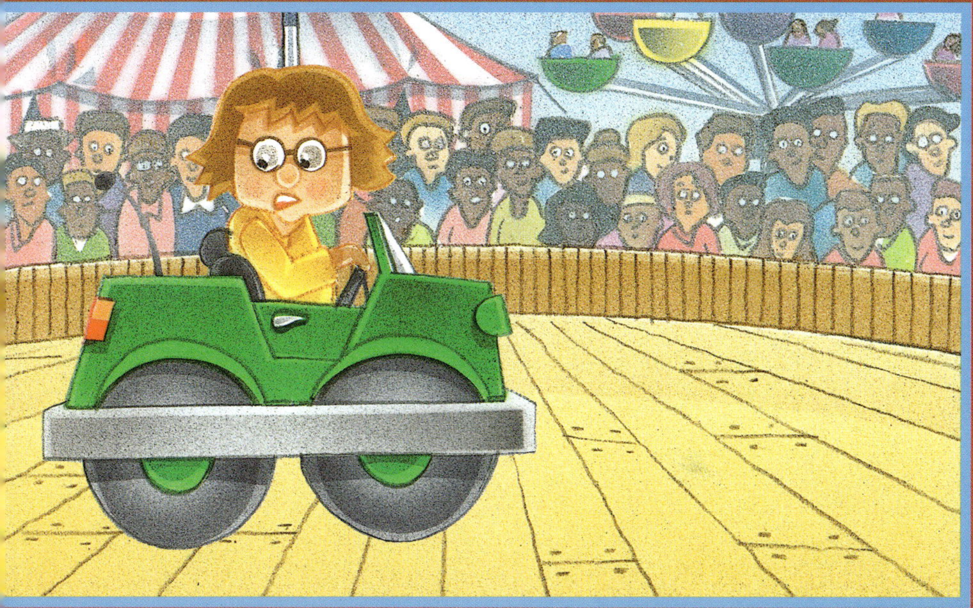

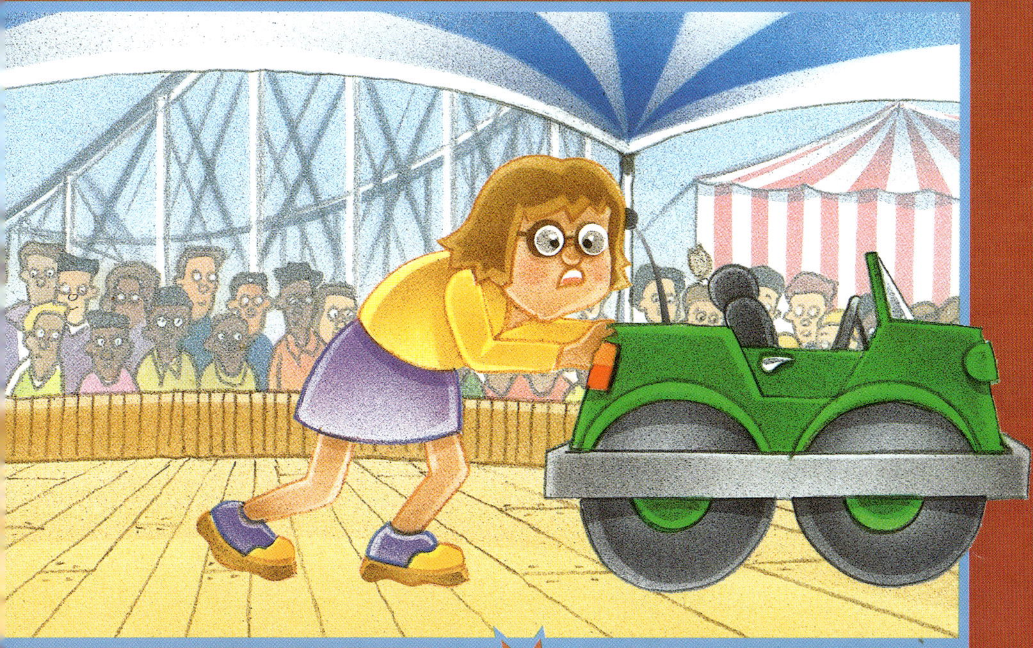

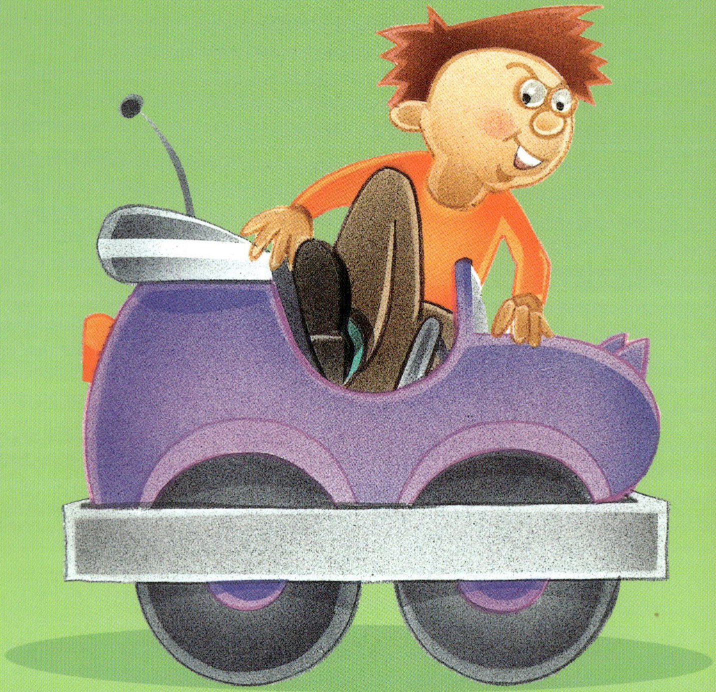

The purple car is for me.

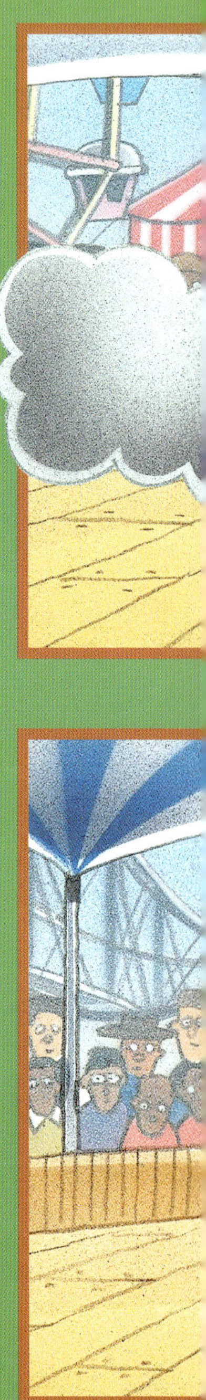

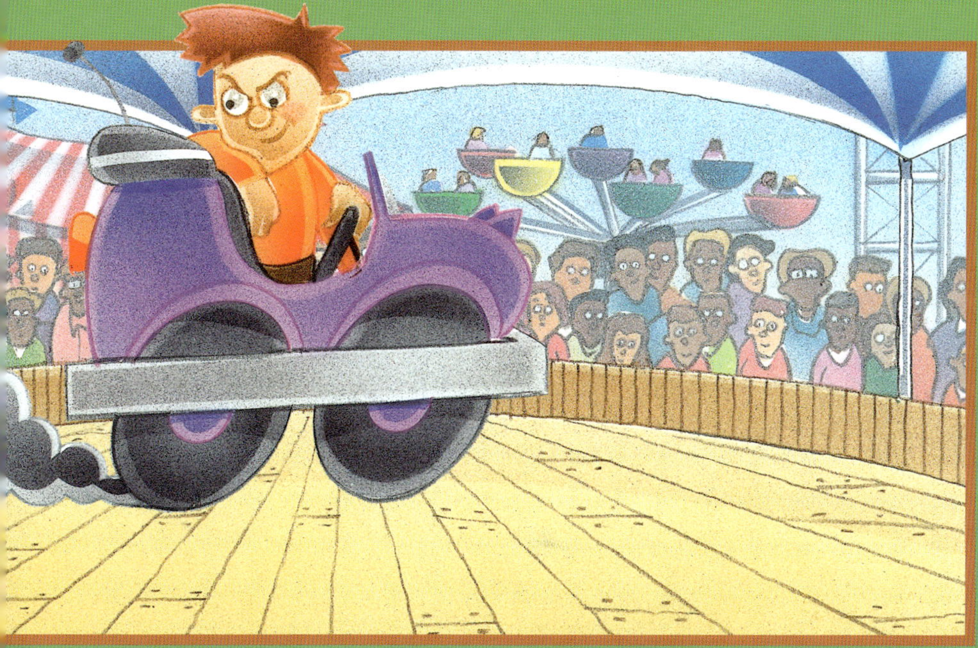

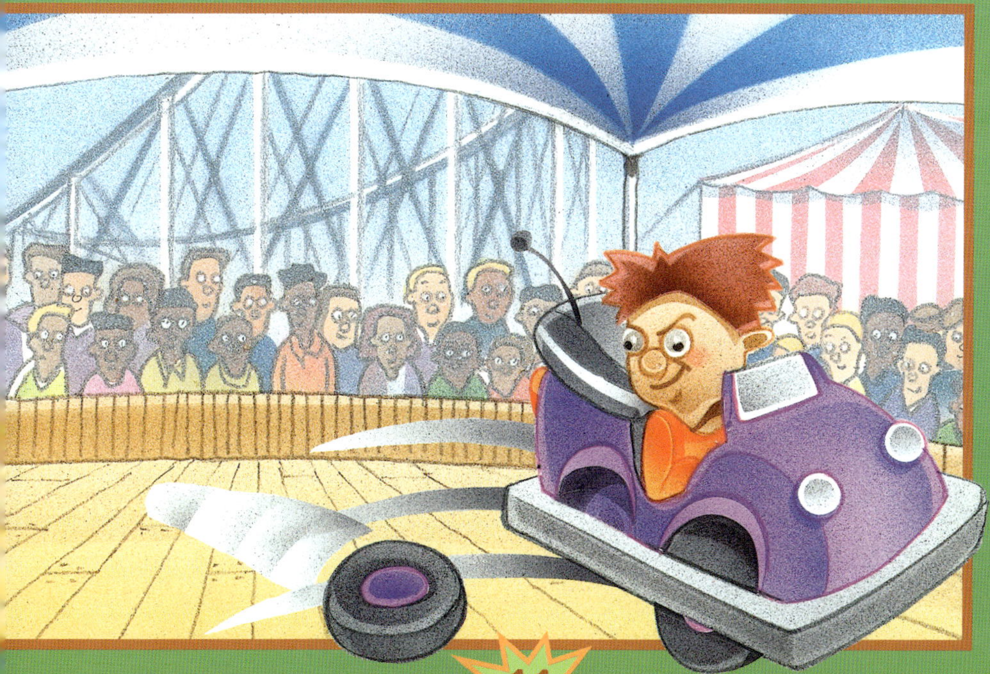

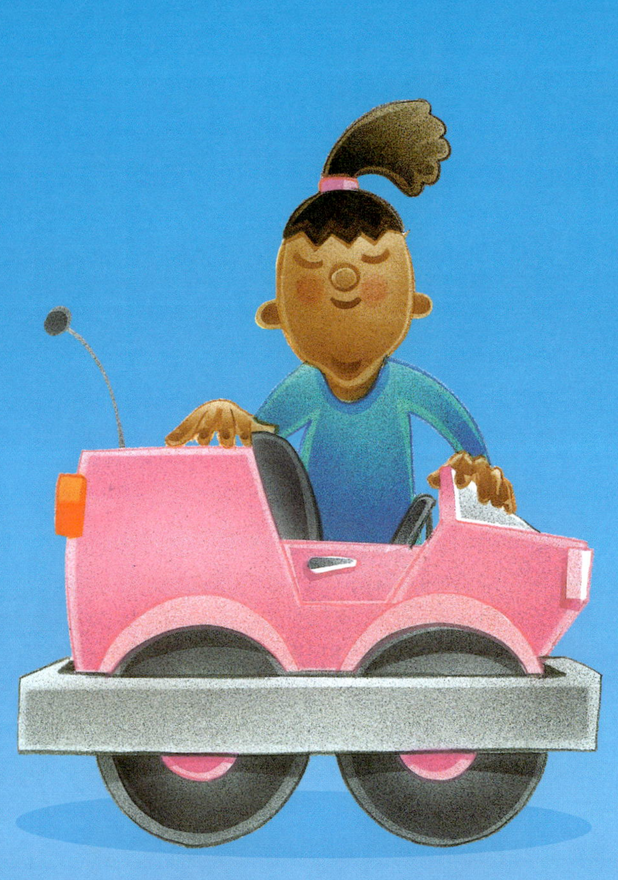

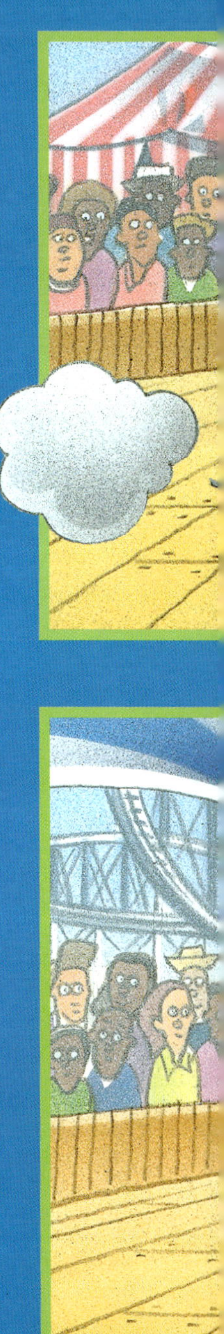

The pink car
is for me.

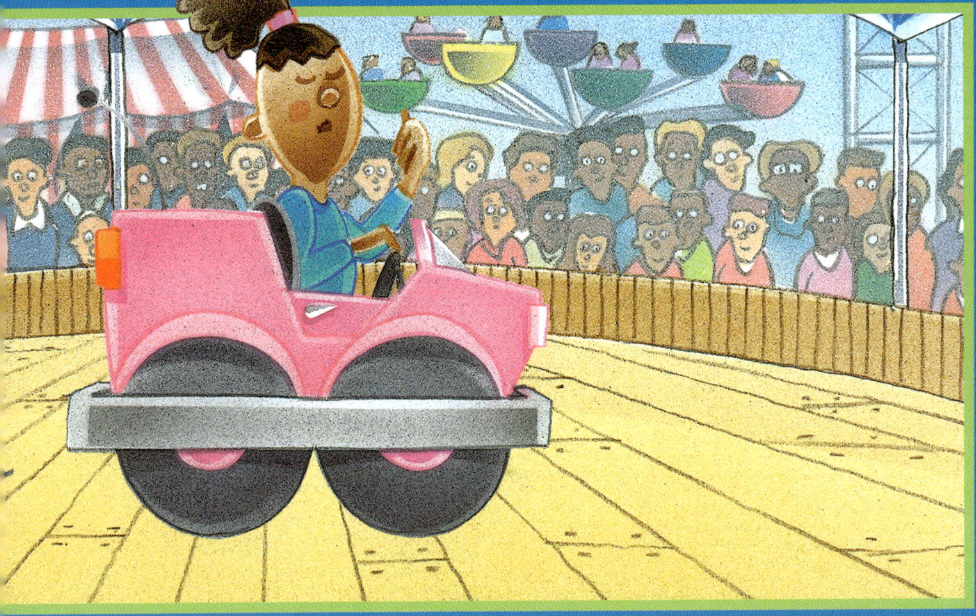

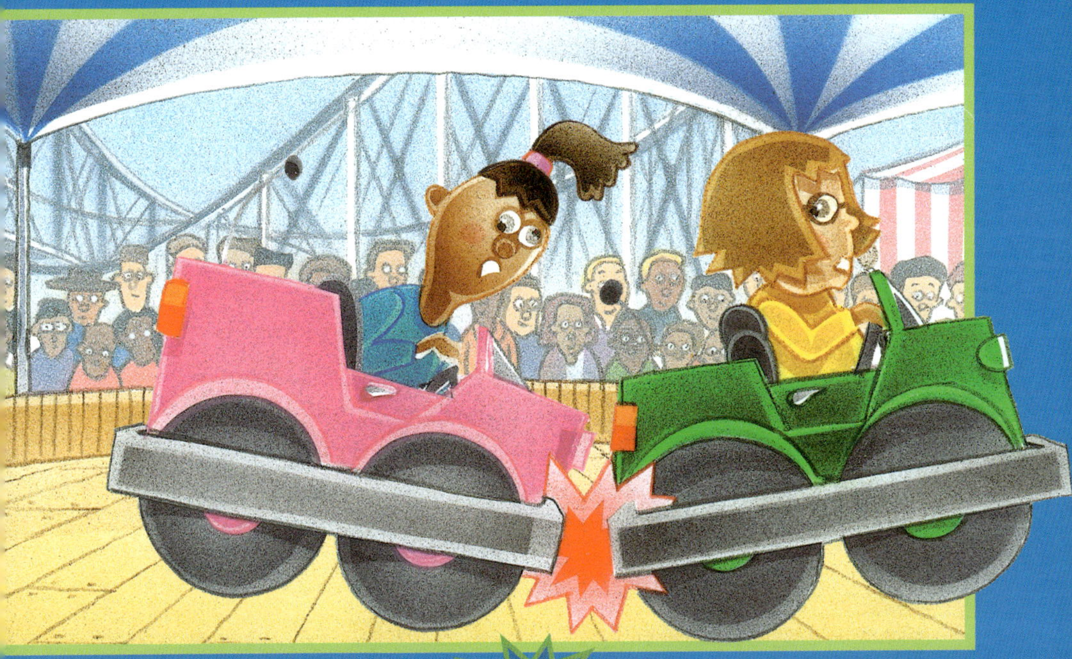

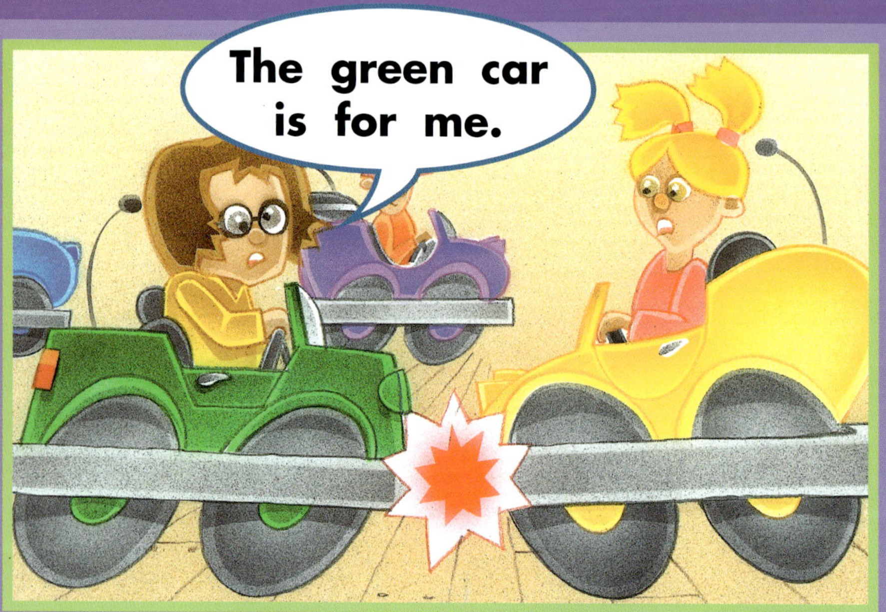
The green car is for me.

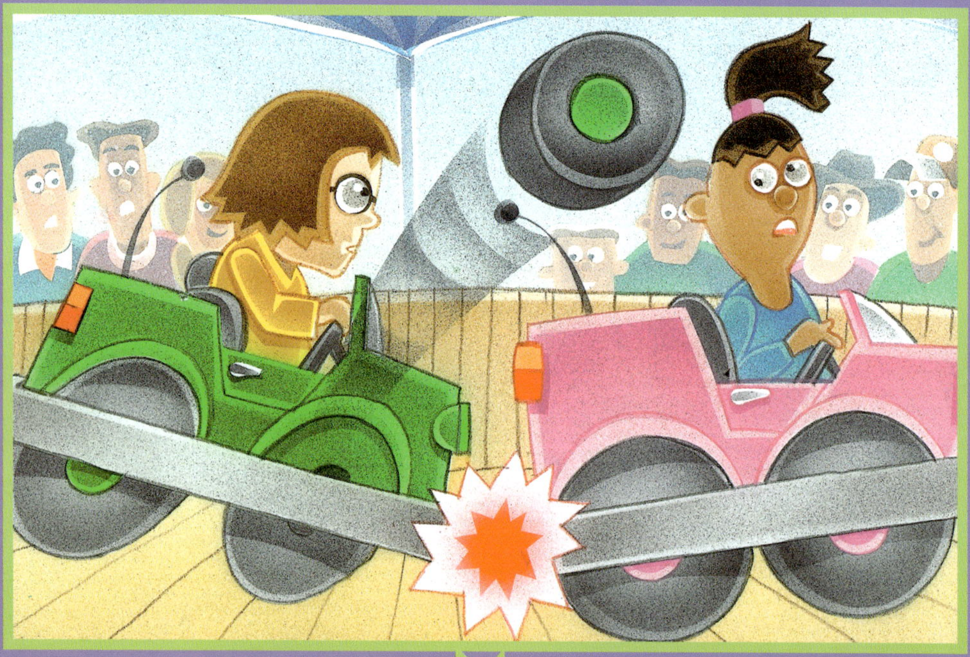

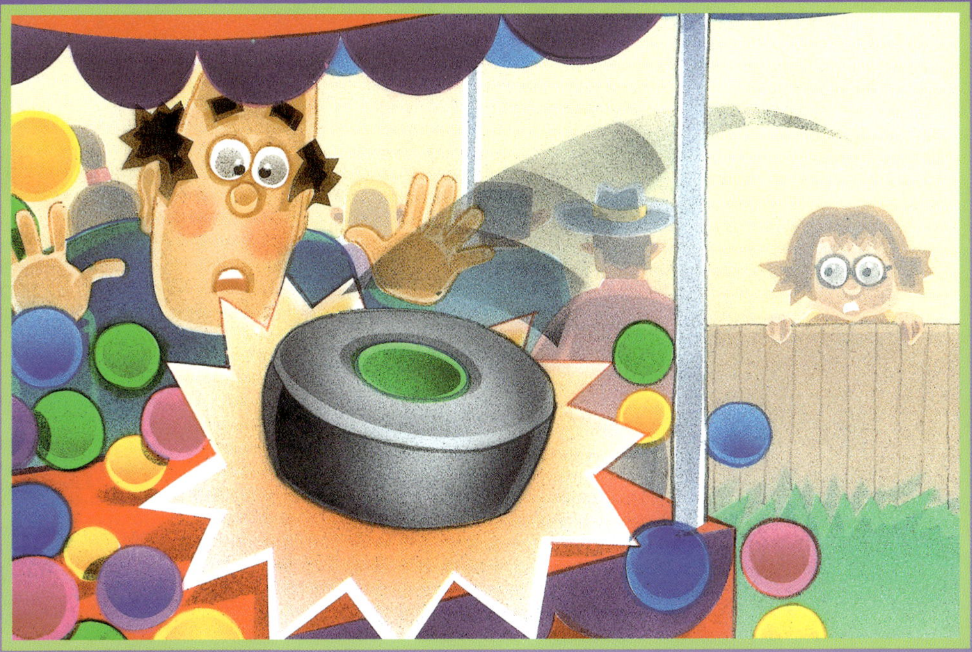

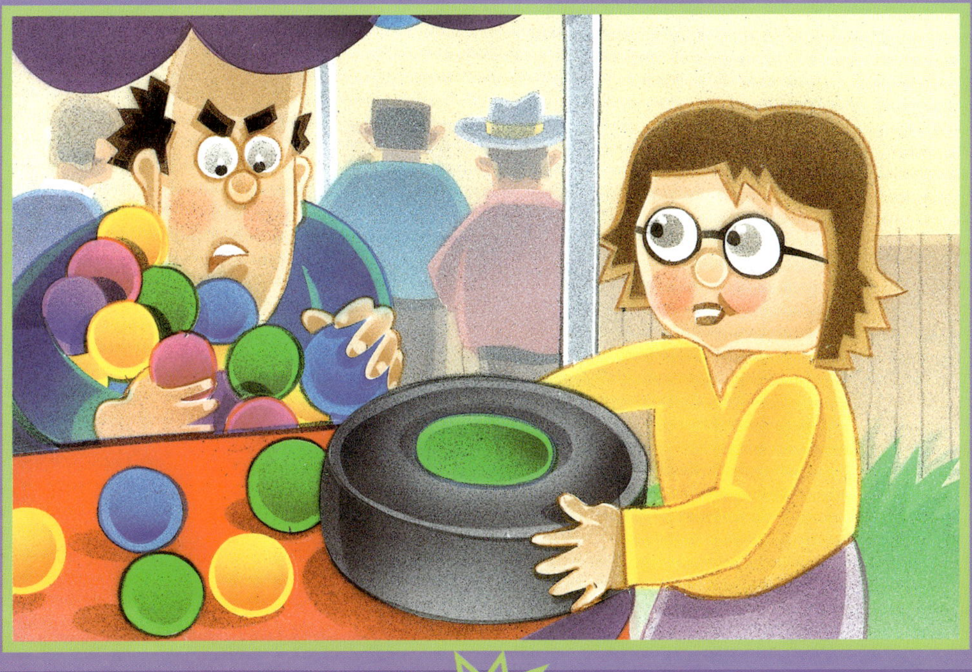

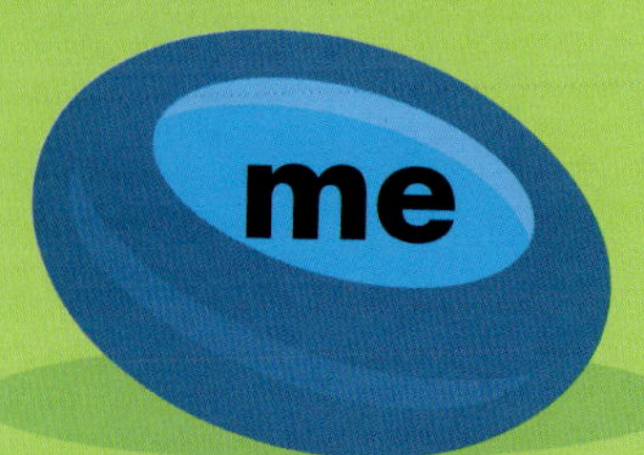

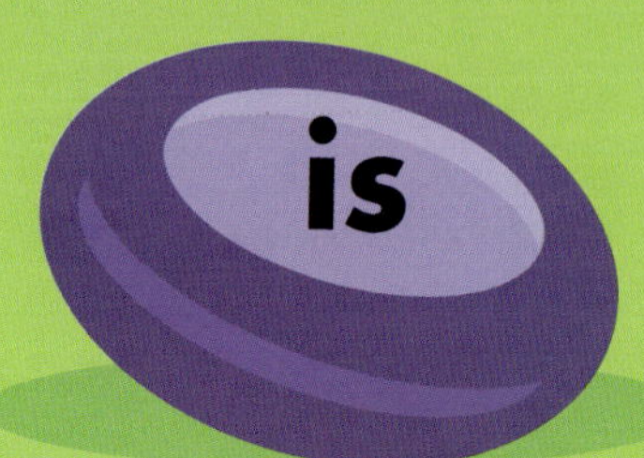

for

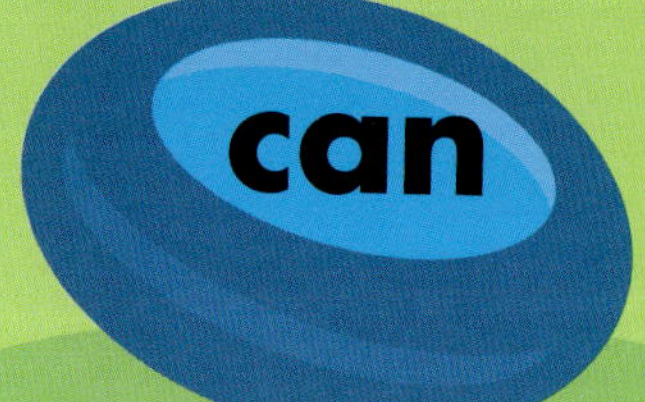

the

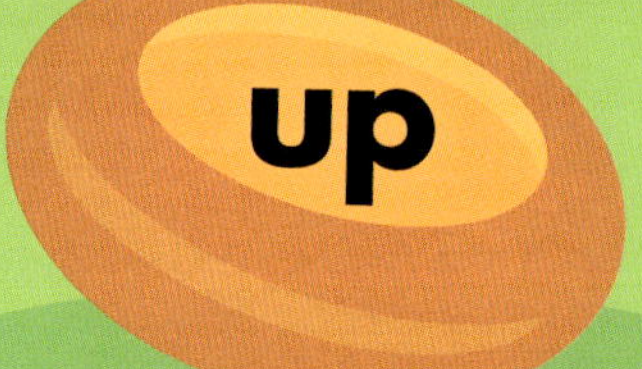

me

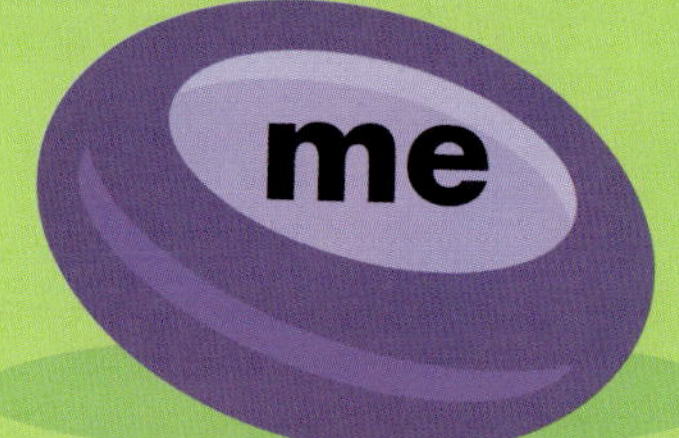

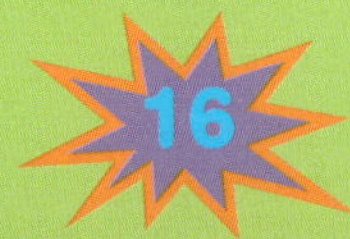